This Book Belongs To

YOUR NAME

Bacteria Joe

By: S Adler

Illustrations: Haim Yafim

English: Rivka Strauss

Just to say "Thank you" for purchasing this book,
I want to give you a FREE gift,
A Flip-Book for your kid.
At the end of this book.

Thank you so much

Sigal Adler

I'm a pretty clean kid,

But I sometimes forget,

Brushing teeth twice a day,

Is really the best bet.

I showered one night,

It was already late,

So brushing my teeth,

I decided could wait.

To my Mom and my Dad,

I wished a good night,

But then I ate chocolate,

Which was not so bright.

That night I had a visit,

From Bacteria Joe,

He's long-nosed and chubby,

And quite hungry you know.

Joe the tooth bacteria,

Sniffed a tempting smell,

The sweet smell of chocolate,

That he loves so well.

He hopped into my mouth,

It was full of sweet stuff,

"I'll invite friends for a party!

There is surely enough."

He started to hum,

Danced a jig with his feet,

He sat down on a tooth,

And he started to eat.

Munching in a dirty mouth,

Joe grew very fat.

He put a lot of pressure,

On the tooth on which he sat.

The sweets were all gone,

From that tooth at the back.

Joe dug for some more,

He nearly made a crack.

Right then I woke up,

Just in the nick of time,

The pain in my tooth,

Was starting to climb.

The bacteria in my mouth,

Saw me start to brush.

He looked at me, worried,

He sang in a rush.

"That toothbrush in your hand, you see,

It really, really troubles me.

Too much toothpaste, give me candy,

Feed me please, that would be dandy.

Your brush won't let me reach my goal,

I want to dig and drill a hole,

I know it hurts you, I don't care,

Please stop now, it's just not fair!"

Surprised, I just stared,

At that singing bacteria,

Then I brushed even more,

To clean the whole area.

Joe's eyes were stinging,

He knew he couldn't stay,

He wiped off the toothpaste,

And quickly ran away.

Ever since that struggle,

I never miss a day,

I brush morning and night,

To prevent tooth decay.

We are very happy that you read our story

This book was written
With lots of love to all my readers.

If you'd like to read more of my children's ebooks,
please Chack my author page on Amazon

http://goo.gl/EDU9W9

Thank you Sigal Adler

Publish and printed in USA, 2014

Please Join My Free Mailing List

And Get A Free flipbook

www.sigaladlerbooks.com

FUN N SUN

17719164R10022

Made in the USA
Middletown, DE
05 February 2015